THE CAT

Or,

How I Lost Eternity

Also by Jutta Richter

The Summer of the Pike

Jutta Richter

THE CAT

Or,

How I Lost Eternity

Translated by

Anna Brailovsky

MILKWEED EDITIONS

© Carl Hanser Verlag München Wien 2006
© 2007, translation by Anna Brailovsky
Milkweed Editions, 1011 Washington Avenue South, Suite 300, Minneapolis, Minnesota 55415.
(800) 520-6455
www.milkweed.org

Published 2007 by Milkweed Editions
Published as *Die Katze* by Carl Hanser Verlag, 2006
Printed in Canada
Author photo by Brigitte Friedrich
Interior illustrations by Rotraut Susanne Berner
07 08 09 10 11   5 4 3 2 1
First Edition

Milkweed Editions, a nonprofit publisher, gratefully acknowledges sustaining support from Emilie and Henry Buchwald; the Bush Foundation; the Patrick and Aimee Butler Family Foundation; CarVal Investors; the Timothy and Tara Clark Family Charitable Fund; the Dougherty Family Foundation; the Ecolab Foundation; the General Mills Foundation; the Claire Giannini Fund; John and Joanne Gordon; William and Jeanne Grandy; the Jerome Foundation; Dorothy Kaplan Light and Ernest Light; Constance B. Kunin; Marshall BankFirst Corp.; Sanders and Tasha Marvin; the May Department Stores Company Foundation; the McKnight Foundation; a grant from the Minnesota State Arts Board, through an appropriation by the Minnesota State Legislature, a grant from the National Endowment for the Arts, and private funders; an award from the National Endowment for the Arts, which believes that a great nation deserves great art; the Navarre Corporation; Debbie Reynolds; the St. Paul Travelers Foundation; Ellen and Sheldon Sturgis; the Target Foundation; the Gertrude Sexton Thompson Charitable Trust (George R. A. Johnson, Trustee); the James R. Thorpe Foundation; the Toro Foundation; Moira and John Turner; United Parcel Service; Joanne and Phil Von Blon; Kathleen and Bill Wanner; Serene and Christopher Warren; the W. M. Foundation; and the Xcel Energy Foundation.

Library of Congress Cataloging-in-Publication Data

Richter, Jutta, 1955–
   [Katze. English]
   The cat, or, how I lost eternity / Jutta Richter ; translated by Anna Brailovsky. — 1st ed.
      p.   cm.
   Originally published: Munich : Carl Hanser Verlag, 2006 under the title, Die Katze.
   Summary: Eight-year-old Christine is late for school every day because a talking alley cat demands her attention, giving her much to think about as he tries to teach her to be spiteful and pitiless.
   ISBN 978-1-57131-676-9 (hardcover)
   [1. Cats—Fiction. 2. Human-animal relationships—Fiction. 3. Schools—Fiction. 4. Conduct of life—Fiction. 5. Germany—Fiction.] I. Brailovsky, Anna. II. Title. III. Title: Cat. IV. Title: How I lost eternity.
   PZ7.R41544Cat   2007
   [Fic]—dc22

                                                                                           2007003917

MINNESOTA
STATE ARTS BOARD

NATIONAL
ENDOWMENT
FOR THE ARTS
A great nation
deserves great art.

For Lilli, Lena, and Perlinus,

for all the cats who know eternity,

and for all children who are wise and kind.

An old white cat lived on our street.

She lived in the sunlight, on the wall right next to the garden gate I passed through on my way to school. I don't know how often I stood there, stroking her head with my hand. I only know that afterward my hand always smelled of fish, which grossed me out. The fishy smell reminded me of Fridays.

That's because Fridays meant fish for dinner—halibut, which made me sick, or maybe herring swimming in blood-red tomato sauce. And I had to sit at the table until my plate was clean.

Of course, the old cat couldn't have known that when she purred at me each morning. Her pale fur was so thin between her eyes and ears that the bare skin shone through. It looked odd, and that summer I often dreamed of bald cats roaming, pink and grubby, through the town.

For another thing, that year I was always late to class, and people started to call me Lollygag Liza. Even when I swore it was the cat's fault, no one believed me.

"You lollygag around," said my father, his eyes bulging in anger.

"You lollygag around," said the teacher, Mr. Hanke, and called me willful. "You are a willful girl," he grumbled.

Oh, yes, willful was what I wanted to be. Utterly willful. A willful girl was like a hen that crowed: something special.

And I was special. A whole world unfolded before me on the street, a world with glimmering, rainbow-streaked gasoline puddles. With red, slimy, naked snails. With pebbles and raspberry bonbons. With bent, rusty nails. With marigolds and caterpillars and this old white cat, who was just as immortal as I was.

Eternity belonged to us.

And eternity began in the shimmering midday heat, when the cat and I stood next to each other and I quietly explained to her the word I had learned that morning.

"You're a willful cat," I whispered, "and I'm a willful girl, and actually, we're magic, and we'll have seventy-seven lives."

"Only seven," purred the cat, "but then who would

believe us? You can't count to seventy-seven; you can't even count to twenty. For you, seventy-seven might as well be a million."

"That's true," I whispered, frightened by the huge numbers. "Do you know how numbers come into our heads?" I asked the cat.

She thought for a while, scouring my hand with her rough little tongue.

"Numbers are determined by the mice," she said finally. "The mice that you've eaten."

"But I've never eaten any mice. Not one, I swear!"

"You'll swear your head off one of these days," the cat hissed, then jumped down from the wall and disappeared behind the garbage cans.

Eternity felt very big and very slow, especially when I couldn't share it with the cat. The only thing that helped was the chain saw that Waldemar Buck used to carve up the afternoon. It wailed over the rooftops, and I imagined that with each wail a little piece of eternity fell from heaven.

Then the sun went down, and my mother threw a sandwich in a plastic bag out the window.

"You can stay outside another half hour!" she shouted.

The streetlamps flickered on. I leaned against a lamppost, chewing and listening to the hum of the electricity.

"How did the electricity get into the lamppost, then?" I asked. But there was no cat to explain it to me.

My father sure couldn't explain it. He only said I'd better quit messing around and do my math homework. But how was I supposed to learn math if I couldn't bring myself to eat mice?

My father didn't have an answer for that either, but instead got those angry, bulging eyes again and called me obstinate.

And so I leaned against the lamppost and brooded, while the old white cat devoured one mouse after another and grew more clever all the time.

Then my parents called me in. I took a bath, combed my hair, and went to bed.

"Good night!" said my mother. "Sweet dreams!"

"Good night, Mama," I answered.

But I dreamed of bald cats roaming through town, and I knew that there weren't any good nights.

2

Waldemar Buck, our neighbor, was a mailman. The cat didn't like him.

Perhaps it was because she thought eternity wouldn't last long if Waldemar Buck kept sawing it apart all afternoon.

But it also could have been because Waldemar Buck kept a German shepherd named Alf in a rusty kennel behind his house. Alf whined a lot, especially on Sundays, when Waldemar Buck went out hunting for a wife.

Waldemar Buck still hadn't found a wife. I suspected he was already much older than my father. Naturally— thanks to the mice—the cat knew exactly how old Waldemar Buck was, but she wasn't telling. "Never mind age," said my mother. "He won't find a wife anyway, thanks to his flat feet."

"Occupational hazard," said my father, then bit into a radish, splitting it in half with his teeth.

It was Sunday evening again, and the German shepherd named Alf was whining.

"That animal should be put to sleep." My mother looked as if she felt sorry for him.

"You remember that," said my father. "An animal is not a toy. You don't let an animal waste away in a rusty kennel."

The cat was actually of the same opinion, but she made an exception for Alf.

"It's his own fault," she hissed. "He licks the hand that beats him instead of biting it. He whines for sympathy in his cage. He attacks when ordered. He lies down on command."

"But there's nothing he can do about it," I said.

"Forget it," hissed the cat. "He's a victim. But he wasn't born a victim. No one is born like that. Every animal is free and strong in the beginning, and the world is always a wonder."

"But if Waldemar Buck locks him up anyway—" I said.

The cat hissed once more, jumped from the wall, and disappeared.

And eternity rose over my head again. I sat on the curb and tried to count the pebbles in the asphalt. If I could make it to thirty, I would understand what the cat meant.

The sun disappeared behind a dark cloud. Just as I got to thirty-two, I discovered a pin with a green-glass head. I picked it up and pricked my finger.

A victim, I thought. A victim means pain. Freely chosen pain. A senseless pain, like a prick from an old, green-headed pin.

And I understood that I could count to thirty-two without eating a single mouse, and that old white cats don't always know everything.

The old white cat appeared suddenly, rubbing up against my back, then putting her head in my hand. "You see," she purred, "you can understand, too, when you make an effort."

3

In the mornings, Waldemar Buck wore his mailman's uniform.

I woke early, at half past five, when the gate in Waldemar Buck's picket fence clattered shut. Then I jumped out of bed, ran to the window, and watched Waldemar Buck, in his dark blue uniform and mailman's cap, shuffling his flat-footed way down the street.

Soon the cat would stall him at the corner by crossing his path and hissing. She knew that Waldemar Buck was superstitious, and crossing his path from left to right was the surest way to ruin his day.

Sometimes, when I stood at the window and watched Waldemar Buck in his uniform getting smaller and smaller until he disappeared at the corner, I thought he was the loneliest person in the world.

And then I resolved to marry him when I grew up.

I'd learn to cook for him, and I'd be waiting for him when he came home tired in the afternoon.

But as soon as this idea came to me, I was frightened. I knew the cat would think I was crazy and never talk to me again.

Loneliness was at least as big as eternity, and who besides the cat knew if you could bear something like that with Waldemar Buck.

"The uniform makes him lonely," said the cat one morning. "People in uniform are always lonely."

"But my mother says it comes from having flat feet," I countered.

"And what do you think?" asked the cat.

"I feel sorry for him," I said. "And it makes me sad to see him in the mornings."

"Sad's not a thought! That's a feeling."

The cat poked her tongue between her lips and suddenly looked idiotic.

"You should never marry for sympathy! And anyway, you can learn to cook on your own, too."

I was startled.

"How do you know I want to marry him?"

"Because you can't do math," grinned the cat, and stuck her tongue back in.

"Girls who can't do math are full of pity, and pitiful girls who can't do math fall in love with lonely uniforms. You're not the least bit willful, you're just dumb!"

4

That morning, Mr. Hanke had had enough.

At half past eleven, he was expecting a total solar eclipse, and we were all supposed to watch. At ten past eleven, Mr. Hanke sent me to the principal's office.

The principal was a very small man—so much smaller than his big, brown claw-foot desk that, in order to see over the top, he must have stuck at least three sofa cushions under his bottom. The claw feet seemed threatening to me at first, but then they began to remind me of something I knew well: cat's feet.

"Well now," said the principal, looking up at me. His small bald head made me think of a baby's.

In his right hand, the principal held a heavy marble ink blotter. I saw his name written twenty times in reverse on the blotting paper; that's how often he had blotted it already today. Maybe he was tired from all that lifting. His fingers could barely reach around the handle.

"Sit down," he said. He set the blotter in front of him on the desk, and its marble spine blocked most of his face. His nose was gone, but his eyes flashed at me.

"You're eight years old, then," he said.

I nodded.

"You're in the third grade."

I nodded.

"You learned to tell time in the first grade."

I nodded.

"Then tell me, what time is it now?" He dangled an old silver pocket watch on a chain in front of my face.

The watch ticked very loudly in the silence.

"Well?"

"It's thirteen minutes past eleven," I answered.

"Right, then," said the principal. "And when does first period start?"

"At a quarter to eight," I answered.

"Can you explain to me why you always come to class so late?"

I nodded.

A vein pulsed angrily on his left temple.

"Then please explain!" hissed the principal.

The room slowly grew dim, and I remembered what

the cat had said: When the sun disappears during the day, time will end.

So the world is about to go under, I thought, and when the world is about to go under, you have to tell the truth.

"It's because of the cat," I heard myself say. "The cat won't let me pass. The cat always wants to talk to me. She needs that in the mornings."

The principal slid down from his sofa cushions and stood before me. He wasn't much bigger standing than he was sitting down, and now he looked like the angry Rumpelstiltskin from my fairy-tale book.

In a minute, I thought, when the world goes under, he will stamp his foot on the ground and be torn in two, and I will never forget it. I will have to dream about it for eternity.

His voice shook with rage as he said: "Your impertinence defies description. As punishment for lying, you will write the following sentence two hundred times: THERE ARE NO TALKING CATS AND IN THE FUTURE I WILL COME TO CLASS ON TIME."

Just as he spoke those words, the room became pitch black. The moon covered the sun. The world went under.

5

When the world returned, I was alone. As usual, Waldemar Buck was sawing up eternity—only this time, I understood the cat's fear that eternity wouldn't last.

I had learned one thing: Even if time stood still and the world went under, sooner or later both would reappear.

"Write your stupid sentences, if you must," the cat hissed. "But it's still betrayal, no matter what!" Then she was gone, and I was left with nothing but the fishy smell on my hand.

The penalty assignment in my backpack weighed on me like a brick. It pushed me down into the asphalt, as if I were sinking into a snowdrift. Every step became a huge effort.

"You shouldn't pick at your food like that," said my mother in an injured tone.

That night, sitting alone in my room, I was afraid of the words.

"I'm warning you," the cat had said. "Once you've written it two hundred times, you'll believe it."

"There are no talking cats," I wrote, and she was right.

I felt sure that something—a secret, a spell—would come to an end. I would lose eternity if I wrote those words.

And if I didn't, Mr. Hanke would force me.

They would lock me up. Lock me in that empty classroom, where it smelled of chalk dust and floor polish. And there I'd sit, without bread and water, all alone. The school would grow quiet. I would listen to the echoing steps of the custodian, hurrying through the empty halls in his gray smock to sell milk to the cleaning ladies. Then the steps of the custodian would fall silent too, and the last thing I'd hear before endless silence descended would be the key turning in the lock after the front door of the school slammed shut.

"There are no talking cats," I wrote.

And suddenly, the solution came to me, as if the old white cat had whispered in my ear.

Waldemar Buck's chain saw wailed, and the cat in my head dictated the right words:

THERE ARE TALKING CATS AND IN THE FUTURE I WILL COME TO CLASS ON TIME.

The punishment couldn't be too bad for a missing word. Even if I had to correct it, I'd only have to add the *no*. A *no* was nothing compared to eternity.

6

I dreamed that night that the cat took me with her for the first time, and together we roamed the dark alleys of the town. She taught me how to balance on roof ridges, how to climb a rusty rain gutter. She taught me to observe the moon and showed me how to stalk mice in the high grass. I crouched next to her, motionless, holding my breath, waiting anxiously for the mouse to move away from its hole—then I sank my claws into the nape of its neck.

I still didn't want to eat the mouse, but that didn't matter tonight, because the cat told me I could manage math some other way.

"You're a natural," she purred softly. And then she said: "I was wrong. You aren't so dumb after all. You really are a willful girl."

Finally, as she led me into the old abandoned house where she lived, the moon tumbled from the sky, and I awoke as the gate slammed shut behind Waldemar Buck.

7

Neither Mr. Hanke nor the principal noticed the missing "no" in my sentences. They were probably too bored to read the same thing two hundred times.

"It's all in the handwriting," said the cat. "Teachers only pay attention to the handwriting. If something looks right and proper, they think what it says is right and proper too. Teachers seldom look carefully."

"But why not?" I asked.

The cat yawned. "Don't you think it's boring to talk about teachers?"

"No," I replied. "Teachers are important. Teachers know everything."

"And that's precisely the problem," said the cat. "Their job is to make disorderly children into orderly students. They always believe they're wiser than our kind. But teachers think only in school years. They have no idea about eternity."

"But you do have to learn things," I argued.

"We learn things in life," said the cat. "In life, what counts are the mice you actually eat."

I suddenly thought of the math problems that I wrote out neatly in my notebook:

A farmer has twenty-six cows. If he takes one-third out to pasture, how many cows remain in the barn?

"Oh," sighed the cat, "show me one single farmer in the whole world who would calculate such nonsense before taking his cows out to pasture!"

I didn't know any farmers, so I decided to spend my afternoons in Nelson's pasture. Fifteen cows grazed there. Surely a farmer would come by eventually and answer my question.

And that's how I learned the language of the cows. I smelled their milk breath in the shimmering afternoon heat. I counted the flies that landed between their shiny, dark brown eyes. I listened to their grass-plucking, lip-smacking sounds.

Those afternoons had no yesterday and no tomorrow— only me and the cows and the cat, who crouched on a fence post and squinted in the sunlight.

8

The Pug lived in the apartment below us.

The Pug was a boy and a head shorter than me, although he was three months older. He had hands like bird claws, gray and scaly. His knuckles were split with bloody cracks. The Pug shuffled when he walked and had three brothers, who were called Fatso, Tall Man, and Shorty. Only the Pug was called the Pug.

"That's what happens when you run out of simple names," said the cat. "Then you take another word that suits. And look at him: doesn't he look like a pug dog?"

I bit my fingernails. Half of me wanted to shake my head.

The other half grinned meanly and nodded. He's disgusting, said the other. He'd better not touch me with his chapped hands, with his claw. And his walk! Rat-Pug, Rat-Pug, my other half called.

"Cut it out," I said. "You can't do anything about being sick."

"But you can do something about names," replied the cat. She hunched her back and sprang from the fence post.

The cows' milk breath suddenly made me sick to my stomach. Eternity became small and hunchbacked, and I stamped my foot.

Get lost! yelled the first half of me. Just get lost, you stupid cat!

The cat hissed and vanished.

My first half whispered in my ear.

You must make friends with him, I heard. You must stand by him.

You must protect him. He's all alone.

"Even more alone than Waldemar Buck?" I asked.

"Even more alone than the humming streetlamp," answered my first half.

I almost burst out crying. I felt sorry for myself as I imagined how pitiful I'd look walking to school hand in hand with the Pug.

We'd take the shortcut over the train tracks, past the slaughterhouse where the pigs screamed, where it smelled of manure, fear, and blood. We'd walk in step together, and if anyone yelled "Pug," I'd throw rocks at them.

It would be winter, I thought, foggy and gloomy. The cat would be sleeping behind some oven, keeping warm.

9

That morning, I was finally at school on time. When the cat had seen me coming, she'd arched her back, hissed, and leapt behind the garbage cans. At first I wanted to call her and say I was sorry for chasing her off. But then I looked straight ahead and simply passed her by. Why should I be the one to apologize? Let her be mad. After all, she started it. She said those things about the Pug.

Mr. Hanke nodded in acknowledgment as I came into the classroom. I had to smile.

You see, hissed the cat in my head, now he's satisfied because he thinks the punishment worked.

In catechism class, Father Wittkamp explained original sin.

It was a quarter to nine, the sun was shining, and late summer sparkled beyond the windows. Father Wittkamp had light blue eyes. In his black suit, he looked like a young jackdaw. He hopped up and down at the front of the room and jerked his head as he spoke.

He said that original sin was Eve's fault, because she listened to the snake and picked the forbidden fruit from the tree. Then she talked Adam into eating it. Of course, the Good Lord noticed it and became so angry that he threw Adam and Eve out of the Garden of Eden. Ever since then, said Father Wittkamp, ever since, every child is born into original sin, for we all come from Adam and Eve.

While he explained this, we drew pictures in our confession books.

The Pug sat next to me in catechism class. He drew a huge black and yellow serpent with crooked fangs. Its jaw gaped and its forked tongue stretched to the margin of the page. I chewed the end of my colored pencil and stared at the serpent. It had really evil eyes.

In the middle of Father Wittkamp's lecture, the Pug tried to hide his picture with one hand while snapping the thumb and forefinger of his other hand.

Father Wittkamp was just coming to baptism.

"It is the holy water that first washes the soul of original sin," he said.

We knew this was a very important point, because his

head jerked two times in a row, his voice shook, and his Adam's apple bobbed up and down as he spoke.

But the Pug didn't quit. He raised his hand and snapped faster and faster.

"Yes, please," Father Wittkamp finally said. "What would you like to tell us, Ferdinand?"

The Pug began to wail.

"Christine is always looking at my picture!" he bawled. "She copies everything from me!"

"That's not true!" I yelled.

"Is too," cried the Pug.

Behind me, Irene Bockmann began to giggle.

Father Wittkamp's face reddened and his Adam's apple twitched.

"But children," he said, wringing his hands. "But children, let's not quarrel!"

Now the whole class was laughing. The Pug, though, kept crying until snot poured from his nose.

Father Wittkamp fluttered helplessly around the room. He took three steps toward the Pug, turned around, flapped his arms, and kept saying: "Now calm down children, calm down now already!"

But we didn't calm down. Just the opposite. Franklin

Wanamaker pulled a rubber band out of his pocket and began to shoot spitballs at the Pug. A mushy, wet little wad of notebook paper hit the Pug right in the middle of his forehead and stuck there.

Father Wittkamp tried to take the rubber band away from Franklin Wanamaker, but Franklin simply jumped up and ran between the desks. Father Wittkamp chased him with great big jackdaw leaps.

We cheered Franklin on and yelled: "Franklin! Franklin! Faster! Faster!"

And the Pug yelled the loudest.

Later, my mother said it had all been because of Father Wittkamp's new black shoes. "Leather soles," she said, "no doubt about it. It was the leather soles. That's quite clear. Leather soles are smooth and dangerous—especially new leather soles on a freshly waxed floor."

Franklin Wanamaker played soccer for the school team. He could fake out and dart sideways, and more importantly, he could run really fast. Long-legged Father Wittkamp was fast, too, especially on the straight stretches between rows of desks—but darting sideways was beyond him, and he had no clue about faking out.

At the end of the second round, he had almost caught

up to Franklin, but Franklin faked like he was going left then darted to the right.

And that's when it happened: Father Wittkamp didn't make the curve. He slipped and crashed.

The classroom fell silent. Father Wittkamp tried to get up, but he couldn't. He fell back on the floor, his face pale and twisted with pain. We had all gathered round and stared at him. He moaned, and then he said: "Children, be good now and go outside, and please get the custodian."

Never had we left our classroom so quietly. We even lined up on our own in two rows and held hands. Only no one wanted to hold hands with the Pug or Franklin Wanamaker.

10

The cat was sitting on the wall, waiting, when I came out of school.

I was happy to see her. Who else could I talk to about Father Wittkamp's accident? Mr. Hanke and the custodian had carried him to the nurse's office on a stretcher. When the ambulance arrived, they loaded Father Wittkamp in and drove away, lights and sirens blaring. During recess, we heard terrible words whispered about *fracture of the femur* and *full cast*. And we waited for our punishment.

But the punishment never came. Mr. Hanke simply went on with the lesson plan and drilled us on the multiplication tables.

The cat loved catastrophes. She listened closely to my story, licked her lips, and grinned.

"That is the punishment," she purred.

"Full cast and a broken leg," she purred.

I was confused.

"What do you mean?"

"Think about it!" said the cat and rubbed her head against my hand.

"What line was he trying to feed you? What was he explaining before it happened?"

"Original sin. Father Wittkamp was explaining original sin. He said the Good Lord was angry because Adam and Eve had eaten the apple from the forbidden tree."

"Well then," purred the cat. "This was the punishment for that!"

"Punishment for what?" I asked.

"For false explanations, of course! Do you really believe that God, the God you call good, would banish mankind from his garden and mark every child ever born with sin just because he didn't want to hand over a single apple?"

"But it was a special apple," I said. "It was an apple from the Tree of Knowledge, after all!"

"You'll talk your head off," hissed the cat. "Do you really believe the Good Lord wants to keep you stupid? But no wonder you think that! You can't even do math!"

She hissed again and jumped from the wall.

And I was confused.

I waited for the wailing of the chain saw, but it didn't come.

I walked down the street and stopped at the Buck fence. Waldemar Buck was stacking wood and the Pug was helping him. They waved at me and I waved back.

All around me the summer air was buzzing, but still, I felt cold. I knew for certain that eternity was over now. And I would never speak with the cat again.

The cat was wicked. She knew no pity. She knew only herself and the mice.

Jutta Richter has written more than twenty books, for which she has won several awards, including the German Youth Literature Award, the Herman Hesse Prize for her body of work, and the Pied Piper's Prize of Hamelyn. She lives in a castle in Münsterland, Germany, and also in Lucca, Tuscany.

Anna Brailovsky has translated numerous works of literature and scholarship, including Fyodor Dostoevsky's *The Idiot*. She lives in Minneapolis, Minnesota.

If you enjoyed this book, you'll also want to read these other Milkweed novels.

To order books or for more information, contact Milkweed at (800) 520-6455 or visit our Web site (www.milkweed.org).

Trudy

Jessica Anderson

MILKWEED PRIZE FOR CHILDREN'S LITERATURE

Aging parents and a new school pose challenges for an eleven-year-old girl.

Perfect

Natasha Friend

MILKWEED PRIZE FOR CHILDREN'S LITERATURE

A thirteen-year-old girl struggles with bulimia after her father dies.

The Summer of the Pike
Jutta Richter

A young girl helps her friends cope with their mother's
illness as they search for the illusive pike.

I Am Lavina Cumming
Susan Lowell

MOUNTAINS & PLAINS BOOKSELLERS ASSOCIATION AWARD

This lively story culminates with the
1906 San Francisco earthquake.

The Linden Tree
Ellie Mathews

MILKWEED PRIZE FOR CHILDREN'S LITERATURE

A moving portrait of life on a 1940s Iowa farm.

A Bride for Anna's Papa
Isabel R. Marvin

Life on Minnesota's Iron Range in the early 1900s.

Minnie
Annie M. G. Schmidt

A cat turns into a woman and helps
a hapless newspaperman.

Behind the Bedroom Wall
Laura E. Williams

Tells a story of the Holocaust through
the eyes of a young girl.

Milkweed Editions

Founded in 1979, Milkweed Editions is one of the largest independent, nonprofit literary publishers in the United States. Milkweed publishes with the intention of making a humane impact on society, in the belief that good writing can transform the human heart and spirit. Within this mission, Milkweed publishes in four areas: fiction, nonfiction, poetry, and children's literature for middle-grade readers.

Join Us

Milkweed depends on the generosity of foundations and individuals like you, in addition to the sales of its books. In an increasingly consolidated and bottom-line-driven publishing world, your support allows us to select and publish books on the basis of their literary quality and the depth of their message. Please visit our Web site (www.milkweed .org) or contact us at (800) 520-6455 to learn more about our donor program.

Typeset in Gill Sans

by Prism Publishing Center.

Printed on acid-free Rolland Natural paper

by Friesens Corporation.